# Mrs. Mog's Cats

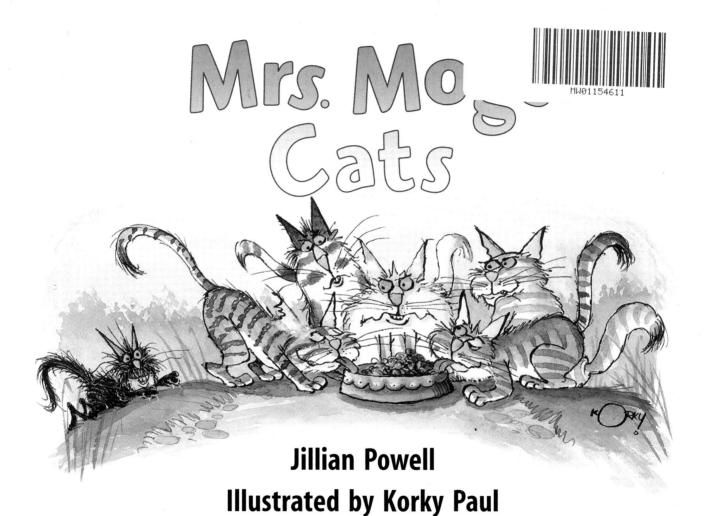

**Jillian Powell**

**Illustrated by Korky Paul**

Rigby

Mrs. Mog has twenty-six cats.
Twenty-six cats has she.
Wherever you look in Mrs. Mog's house,
a cat is sure to be.

You see
cats at the window,
and cats at the door.

Cats on the ceiling,
and cats on the floor.

You see cats in the bathroom and cats in the bed.

Cats in the kitchen,
and cats being fed.

There are cats by the beehive
chasing the bees.

There are cats on the rooftops,
and cats in the trees.

You see cats out hunting.

There goes a mouse!

You see cats on the doorstep,
and a mouse in the house!

Mrs. Mog has twenty-six cats.

Twenty-six cats has she.

Wherever you look in Mrs. Mog's house,

a cat is sure to be.